Classic Cornish Ghost Stories

Compiled by Paul White

Tor Mark Press   Penryn

The Tor Mark series

Introduction

'Of all the vulgar superstitions of the half educated, none dies harder than the absurd delusion that there is no such thing as ghosts.' So wrote the American journalist WT Stead (who was later unfortunate enough to choose the *Titanic* for his return passage), making a tongue-in-cheek introduction to a book of ghost stories.

Neither belief nor disbelief in ghosts is required of the reader of this book: it is a collection of stories from some of the major sources of Cornish history and folklore, and some of the authors quoted are themselves clearly sceptical. But belief in spirits and supernatural events was a pervasive feature of past times in Cornwall – and indeed in most other parts of Britain – and if you are not content with just a good read, you can regard these stories as evidence of our ancestors' state of mind, or as evidence for actual visitation by apparitions.

The main sources are the Victorian folklorists William Bottrell, MA Courtney, Rev. CA Johns and Robert Hunt (although most of his ghost stories are contained in other books in this series); contributors to *The Arminian Magazine*, *Cornubiana*, *The Cornish Magazine* and *Old Cornwall*; the writers Jonathan COuch, Samuel Drew, AS Oates and J Polsue, and the exhilaratingly unreliable Rev. Sabine Baring-Gould.

For the most part the extracts have been left unedited, except for occasional modernisation of pronunciation.

First published 1994 by Tor Mark Press
Islington Wharf, Penryn, Cornwall TR10 8AT
This reprint 1996

© 1994 Tor Mark Press

ISBN 0-85025-344-6

Acknowledgements
The cover illustration is by Linda Garland.
Printed in Great Britain by Burstwick Print and Publicity Services, Hull

The tragedy of sweet William and fair Nancy

Far back in old times, the son of a fisherman who dwelt in Pargwarra lived many years — off and on from a boy — in service with a rich farmer in Roskestal, and courted his master's only daughter, who, almost from her childhood, loved the young serving-man with a strength of affection beyond her control.

The youngster, being of a roving turn, often went to sea for many months in summer, and although he was most wanted on the farm, his master always took him back again when sailors were paid off and merchants laid up during the stormy winter season. It was his old master's and Nancy's great delight of winter's nights to be seated with neighbours around the fire and hear Willy tell of strange things he had beheld on the ocean and in foreign lands; they wondered at what he related of water-spouts, icebergs, and northern lights, of whales, seals, and Laplanders. And they listened with awe and surprise to what he told them of burning mountains, where he said he had seen, from a distance, the very mouths of hell vomiting clouds of sulphurous smoke, flames, and rivers of fire. And when sailing as near these dreadful regions as anyone dared venture for the heat, and for fear of having their vessel drawn ashore, where all the nails would be pulled from her planks by the lodestone rocks that bordered these lands, of nights he had heard, high overhead, devils shouting, 'The time is come but such and such a one isn't come.' Soon after one would hear doleful cries and behold black clouds of doomed spirits driven to the burning mountains by troupes of demons.

He had seen the wreck of Pharoah's chariots on the beach of the Red Sea, which, he assured them, had retained the hue from which it took its name ever since the Egyptian hosts were slain and overwhelmed, where their bones are still bleaching on the sands.

But all that was easily believed by his simple hearers and mere nothing to the marvels he related from shipmates' stories, when he told them of those bold mariners who had been farther east and seen the Dead Sea across which no bird could fly — how they had plucked from trees that bordered its black waters apples full of ashes that were tempting to the eye; they had touched Lot's wife turned to salt, and brought home some of her fingers; that was often done, he said, for with the next tide's flow they sprouted out again.

The neighbours liked above all to hear him tell about the dusky men and strange women of Levantine lands, and how the latter would shoot loving glances at British tars through peepholes cut in their thick black cloth veils.

Now William himself was a wonder of perfection, past compare in Nancy's eyes. She admired him for his stalwart form, for his strange adventures on sea and land, and for the rare presents he brought her home. The farmer, too, liked him just as if he had been his own son, yet it never entered his head that his daughter and only child would ever think of the dashing and careless young seaman as her lover.

Yet her mother, more sharp sighted, soon discovered that her fair Nancy was much in love with their serving-man. When William was gone to sea the dame upbraided her with want of proper pride and self respect till she had fretted her almost to death's door. 'What a fool thou must be,' said she, 'to throw thyself away, or to hanker after one so much beneath thy degree, when thy good looks and dower make thee a match for the richest farmer's son in the West Country; think if you wed a poor sailor how you will be scorned by all your kith and kin.'

Nancy replied, 'But little care I for relations' reproach or good will; sink or swim, if ever I marry it shall be the man I love who is able to work and win.' The dame prevailed upon her husband, much against his will however, not to take the sailor to live there when he returned home again; and she — watching her opportunity — slammed the door in his face and told him he should never more harbour beneath her roof.

But the father, fearing his only child would pine to death, told her and her lover that if he would try his fortune by a voyage to the Indies or elsewhere for three years, when he returned, poor or rich, if he and Nancy were of the same mind they might be wedded for all he cared.

That being agreed on, William got a berth in a merchant-man bound for a long voyage, took friendly leave of his old master, and the night before his ship was ready to sail he and Nancy met, and he assured the sorrowing damsel that in three years or less she might expect him to land in Pargwarra with plenty of riches, and he would marry at home or fetch her away and make her his bride.

They vowed again and again to be constant and true; with their hands joined in a living spring or stream, they broke a gold ring in two between them, each one keeping a part. And to make their vows more binding, they kindled at dead of night a fire on the Garrack Zans [holy rock] which then stood in Roskestal town place and, joining their hands over the flame, called on all the powers of heaven and earth to witness their solemn oaths to have each other living or dead. Having plighted their troth with these and other ancient rites — that romantic lovers of old regarded as more sacred than a marriage ceremony — they said farewell and William went on his way and joined his ship.

Three years passed during which the old dame did her utmost to persuade her daughter to become the wife of some rich farmer — for true it was, as she said, that Nancy might have had her choice of the best — yet coaxing and reproaches were powerless to shake the maid's constancy. When three years and many months were gone without any tidings of William, she became very melancholy — perhaps crazy — from hope deferred, and took to wandering about the cliffs in all weathers, by day and by night.

On the headland called Hella Point, which stretches far out west of the cove, there is a high overhanging rock almost on the verge of the cliff, which shelters on its southern side a patch of greensward mostly composed of cliff pinks; this spot used to be known as Fair Nancy's bed. There she would pass hours by day and often whole nights watching vessels that came within her ken, hoping to see her lover land from every one that hove in sight, and to be the first to hail him with joyful greetings in the cove. Her father and the old fisherman — anxious for William's return — treated her as tenderly as a shorn lamb, and often passed long nights with her there. At length the poor maiden had to be watched and followed for fear that in her night wanderings she might fall over the cliff or drown herself in a fit of despair.

One moonlit winter's night, when in her chamber indulging her grief, she heard William's voice just under her window, saying, 'Sleepest thou, sweetheart? Awaken and come hither, love; my boat awaits us at the cove, thou must come this night or never be my bride.'

'My sweet William come at last! I'll be with thee in an instant,' she replied.

Nancy's Aunt Prudence, who lodged in the same room, heard Willy's request and his sweetheart's answer; looking out of her window she saw the sailor, just under, dripping wet and deathly pale. An instant after — glancing round into the chamber and seeing Nancy leave it — she dressed in all haste and followed her. Aunt Prudence, running down the cliff lane at her utmost speed, kept the lovers in sight some time, but couldn't overtake them, for they seemed to glide down the rocky pathway leading to Pargwarra as if borne on the wind, till they disappeared in the glen.

At the fisherman's door however, she again caught a glimpse of them passing over the rocks towards a boat which floated off in the

cove. She then ran out upon the How, as the high ground project-
ing into the cove is called, just in time to see them on a large flat
rock beside the boat, when a fog rolling in over the sea shrouded
them from her view. She hailed them but heard no reply.

In a few minutes, the mist cleared away, bright moonlight again
shone on the water, but the boat and lovers had disappeared.

Then she heard mermaids singing a low, sweet melody and saw
many of them sporting on the water under Hella; that was nothing
new however, for the rocks and caves bordering this headland were
always noted as favourite resorts of these death-boding syrens, whose
wild unearthly strains were wont, before tempests, to be heard
resounding along Pedn-Penwith shores.

By daybreak the old fisherman came to Roskestal and told the
farmer that he hoped to find his son there, for, about midnight, he
saw him at his bedside looking ghastly pale; he stayed but a moment
and merely said, 'Farewell father and mother, I am come for my
bride and must hasten away.' Then he vanished like a spirit. It all
seemed to the old man uncertain as a dream; he didn't know whether
it were his own son in the body or a token of his death.

In the afternoon, ere they had ceased wondering and making
search for Nancy, a young mariner came to the fisherman's dwelling,
and told him that he was chief officer of his son's ship, then at the
Mount with a rich cargo from the Indies, bound for another port;
but put in there because his son — her captain — when off Pargwarra
where he intended to land last night, eager to see his native place,
went aloft and the ship rolling he missed his holdfast on the shrouds,
fell overboard and sank before the ship could be brought to or
any assistance rendered.

All knew then that it was William's ghost which had taken Nancy
to a phantom boat and a watery grave was the lovers' bridal-bed.
Thus their rash vows, of constancy even in death, were fulfilled, and
their sad story for a time caused Pargwarra to be known as the
Sweethearts' Cove, and some will have it that the old Cornish name
has that meaning.

The doom of Sir Cloudesley Shovel

Sir Cloudesley Shovel was a successful admiral but is now generally remembered only for the disaster which befell him in 1707, when
his fleet was wrecked on the Isles of Scilly in a great storm and Sir
Cloudesley himself was presumed drowned. In fact he was mur-
dered by an inhabitant as he lay helpless on the shore, for the sake
of his possessions.

A few days previously, one of the sailors on the flagship, himself a Scillonian, so persistently and clamorously warned the officer of the watch that the fleet was heading for the rocks that the admiral found him guilty of insubordination, and had him hanged at the yard-arm.

Before his public execution, the sailor begged to be allowed to read aloud one of the psalms, and read Psalm 109 with much emphasis on the curses, and then predicted a watery grave for Sir Cloudesley. The weather had been fair but as the body was committed to the deep, the wind began to blow and his ship-mates were horrified to see the corpse, freed of its winding sheet, face up and following in their wake. Even before the vessel struck, they gave themselves up for lost men.

The Ghosts of Chapel Street and St Mary's Yard, Penzance

Little more than fifty years ago [this was written in the 1860s], the building in Chapel Street which now serves as a dispensary, with the adjoining house at the entrance to Vounderveor Lane, formed a mansion which belonged to and was occupied by an elderly lady, Mrs Baines. At that time there was, at the rear of this mansion, a large garden or rather orchard and garden, extending westward nearly to New Road and bounded on the south by Vounderveor. The south side of the lane was an open field, and at its west end there were no dwellings. Where the School of Art, the Methodist vestries and other houses stand, was all known as Mrs Baines' orchard. This pleasant spot, in which the lady took great delight, was stocked with the choicest apple, pear, plum and other fruit trees then known. The town boys soon found out the flavour of Mrs Baines' fruit, which was to them all the sweeter for being stolen. When the apples were ripe and most tempting, the mistress and her serving man watched the garden by turns — the man during the first part of the night, and madam would descend in her night dress every now and then, to see that all was right, in the small hours of the morning.

One night Mrs Baines, suspecting that man Jan was rather careless in keeping guard, sallied forth to see if he was attending to his duty; and not finding him anywhere about the garden, she went to a tree of highly prized apples and shook down a good quantity, intending to take them away and thus prove to Jan that, through his remissness, the fruit was stolen. But her man Jan, armed with an old blunderbuss charged with peas and small shot, was at no great distance, dozing under a hedge. The rustling of shaken branches and noise of falling apples awoke him and, seeing somebody as he

7

thought stealing apples from their favourite tree, he up with his gun and let fly at his mistress, exclaiming at the same time, 'Now you thief, I've paid 'e off for keeping me out of bed to watch 'e! I know 'e I do, and will bring 'e before his worship the mayor tomorrow!'

'Lord help me, I'm killed!' cried the lady, as she fell on the ground. Jan stayed to see no more, but, frightened out of his wits, ran away and couldn't be found for several days. At last he was discovered up in Castle-an-Dinas, half starved. By good luck the old lady's back was towards her man when he fired, and the greatest portion of the charge took effect below her waist. Doctor Giddy was fetched, and after some delicate surgical operations which the lady bore with exemplary patience, pronounced her fright to be more than her hurt.

However, a short time after the old lady got shot, she died; and then she kept such ward and watch over her orchard that few were so bold as to enter, after day-down, into the haunted ground where the ghost of Mrs Baines was often seen under the tree where she was shot, or walking the rounds of her garden. Everybody knew the old lady by her upturned and powdered grey hair under a lace cap of antique pattern; by the long lace ruffles hanging from her elbows; her short silk mantle, gold headed cane, and other trappings of old-fashioned pomp. There are many still living in Penzance who remember the time when they wouldn't venture on any account to pass through Vouderveor Lane after nightfall, for fear of Mrs Baines' ghost. Sometimes she would flutter up from the garden (just like an old hen flying before the wind) and perch herself on the wall; then, for an instant, one might get a glimpse of her spindle legs and high heeled shoes before she vanished.

Her walking in the garden might have been put up with, but she soon haunted all parts of the premises and was often seen where least expected both by night and by noon-day. The ghost became so troublesome at last that no person could be found to occupy the house, where she was all night long tramping about from room to room, slamming the doors, rattling the furniture, and often making a fearful crash amongst glass and crockery. Even when there was no living occupant in the house, persons standing in Chapel Street often saw through the windows a shadowy form and lights glimmering in the parlours and bedrooms.

The proprietors, driven to their wits' end, unwilling that such valuable property should become worse than useless, at last sent for a parson who was much famed in this neighbourhood as an exorcist (we think the name of this reverend ghost-layer was Singleton), that he might remove and lay the unresting spirit; and he succeeded (by what means our informant knows not) in getting her away down to the sandbanks on the Western Green, which were then spread over many acres of land where the waves now roll. Here this powerful parson, single handed, bound her to spin from the banks ropes of sand for the term of a thousand years, unless she before that time spun a sufficiently long and strong one to reach from St Michael's Mount to St Clement's Isle. The encroaching sea having swept away the sandbanks, Mrs Baines ghost is probably gone with them, as she hasn't been heard of for some years and, if she returns, the present occupiers of the house wouldn't mind her.

Long after parson Singleton laid the old lady's ghost, many persons were deterred from taking the house because there was a story current that the spirit was confined to a closet in some out-of-the-way part of the house, and that the door of this ghost's place was walled up and plastered over, yet the sound of her spinning wheel was frequently heard in the upper regions of the old house.

About the time that Mrs Baines' ghost carried on its freaks in the mansion, an open pathway passed through St Mary's chapel-yard, which was then often crossed as it shortened the distance to the Quay; but for a long time few persons liked to pass through the burial ground at night because a ghostly apparition, arrayed in white, was often seen wandering amongst the tombs, from which doleful sounds were frequently heard. Sometimes the fearful figure was also met on the path or in the chapel porch. One dark and rainy night, however, a sailor who neither knew nor cared anything about the ghost of St Mary's, in taking the short cut through the chapel yard came as far as the chapel porch when the ghost issued forth on the path and there stood, bobbing it head and waving its shroudings before him.

'Holloa! who or what are you?' said the sailor.

'I am one of the dead,' the ghost answered.

'If you are one of the dead, what the deuce are you doing above ground? Go along down below!' said the sailor, as he lifted his fist and dealt the ghost a stunning blow over its head, which laid it sprawling on the stones, where it remained some time, unable to rise or descend, until a person passing by assisted it to get on its legs and discovered that a frolicsome gentleman called Captain Carthew, who then lived in the house which is now Mrs Davy's property, had long been diverting himself and frightening the townsfolk out of their wits by personating the ghost, which was most effectually laid by the jack tar, and served out for its tricks on the timid and the credulous.

This story is taken verbatim from *Traditions and Hearthside Stories of West Cornwall*, by William Bottrell (Penzance 1870), but Eric Hirth in his *Ghosts in Cornwall* (St Ives 1986) reports continued activity from Mrs Baines in the 1980s, at the Peninsula Restaurant.

The coach with headless horses

Another apparition feared in Penzance was an old-fashioned coach drawn by headless horses, which rumbled through the streets; on those same nights could also be seen a procession of coffins, wending its way to the churchyard. To see either of these was most unlucky, as a death in the family was bound to follow shortly thereafter, and one woman who was so unfortunate as to brush against the spectral coach died that very night. The coach, or another like it, was also seen at Penryn, just before Christmas, and here the coachman had the power of spiriting away people who stared at him, unless they knew mystical signs by which to avert the evil.

The Leeds Town Ghost

Leeds Town is a hamlet inland from Breage; the ghost runs up and down stairs in a particular house during the night and then sits in a corner of the room weeping and sleeking her hair. It is the ghost of a young woman who was engaged to be married to a man who refused to become her husband until she gave him certain deeds kept in a box in this room. As soon as the deeds were in his possession he sold off the property and escaped to America, leaving the luckless girl to bemoan her loss. She went mad; night and day she was searching for her deeds; sometimes she would sit and wail in the spot where the box had been. At length she died; her spirit however had no rest and constantly returns to keep alive the memory of man's perfidy.

Thomas Flavel, ghost layer

Thomas Flavel, who died in 1682, attained during his life great celebrity for his skill in the questionable art of laying ghosts. His fame still [written about 1890] lingers in the memories of the more superstitious of the inhabitants through the following ridiculous stories. On one occasion when he had gone to church his servant girl opened a book in his study, whereupon a host of spirits sprang up all round her. Her master observed this, though then occupied at church, closed his book and dismissed the congregation. On his return home he took up the book with which his servant had been meddling and read backwards the passage which she had been reading, at the same time laying about him lustily with his walking cane, whereupon all the spirits took their departure, but not before they had pinched the servant girl black and blue.

His celebrity, it seems, was not confined to his own parish for he was once called upon to lay a very troublesome ghost in an adjoining parish. As he demanded the large fee of five guineas for his services, two of the persons interested resolved to assure themselves by the evidence of their own eyes that the ceremony was duly performed. They accordingly, without apprising the other of their intention, secreted themselves behind two graves in the churchyard a short time before the hour named for the absurd rites. In due time the ghost layer entered it with a book in one hand and a horsewhip in the other. On the first smack of the whip the watchers raised their heads simultaneously, caught a glimpse of each other, and were both so terrified that they scampered off in opposite directions, leaving the operator to finish his business as he might.

In olden times there were several of these ghost laying clergymen in Cornwall. One was the Rev. Mr Woods of Ladock, who when walking usually carried an ebony stick with a silver head on which was engraved a pentacle, and on a broad silver ring below planetary signs and mystical figures.

Mr Woods was usually a match for most demons, whom he would change into animals and thrash with his whip; but one more cunning than the rest defied him, by taking the shape of an unknown coal-black bird and perching on the church tower, from whence during divine service he made all sorts of queer noises, disturbing the congregation and inciting the irreverent to laughter. He was too high up to be exorcised or reached with the whip. At last the clergyman, at his wit's end, remembered that the Evil One could not endure the sight of innocent children, and he sent his clerk round to all the mothers of his parish who had unchristened children, asking them to bring them to church the next Sunday to have the rite performed. As he was a great favourite with his people all the mothers, and they were eight, readily agreed to come. But as twelve is the mystical number he invited four other mothers whose children had recently been baptised to come as well and bring their children and sponsors with them.

The eight children were christened, and the parson walked out of church followed by the twelve mothers with the infants in their arms. The clerk arranged them in lines five deep, the mothers in front, opposite the belfry tower. Mr Woods directed each to pass her child from one to the other of its sponsors, and then hand it to him that he might hold it up for the demon to see; but for some time the cunning bird hid himself behind a pinnacle and nothing would induce him to look, until one of the children, growing tired, began to cry and all the others chimed in, screaming in chorus at the top of their voices. Then the demon hopped down from his perch and peered over the parapet to try and find out what could be the matter. The sight of the twelve children had such an effect upon him that he too gave an unearthly yell and flew away never to reappear. The church bells were soon after put in order, and it is well known that no evil spirit ever ventures within sound of their ringing.

Willy Willcock's hole

Behind the quay at Polperro, and in the side of the hill, is a cavern known as Willy Willcock's hole, which was believed by the fisher boys to extend into the hill to a distance directly under Landaviddy. Many years ago, Willy Willcock, determined to test the truth of this opinion, crept with difficulty through the narrow opening at the back of this cave and got entangled in its inner mazes. He was never afterwards seen, but the shrieks of his disturbed ghost are yet plainly to be heard in the hill after nightfall.

A Wesley ghost story

When John Wesley visited St Agnes on one of his many preaching missions, he was able to obtain accommodation only in an ancient mansion which was unoccupied because haunted by ghosts.

Wesley went to the house and sat up reading by candlelight. At midnight he heard a noise in the hall and, on issuing from his room, saw that a banquet was spread and that richly apparelled ladies and gentlemen were about the board. Then one cavalier, with dark piercing eyes and a pointed black beard, wearing a red feather in his cap, said: 'We invite you to eat and drink with us,' and pointed to an empty chair.

Wesley at once took the place indicated, but before he put in his mouth a bite of food or drank a drop, said: 'It is my custom to ask a blessing; stand all!' Then the spectres rose.

Wesley began his accustomed grace, 'The name of God, high over all — ' when suddenly the room darkened and all the apparitions vanished.

The same story, however, is told of a commercial traveller at St Austell....

Parson Jago and the suicide's ghost

On a bleak road between Helston and Wendron Church-town, at its highest and wildest spot about a third of a mile from the church, three roads meet. Here at Three Cross, or Wendron Cross as it is variously known, two hundred and more years ago when the road was unmade and the Downs unenclosed and it was far more desolate even than now, a poor suicide named Tucker was buried. Few liked to pass up Row's Lane after nightfall for there Tucker's shade had more than once been seen. One man however, valiant in his cups on his return from Helston market, cracked his whip and shouted lustily, 'Arise, Tucker!' as he passed the place.

It is said Tucker did arise, and fixed himself on the saddle behind the man as he rode on horseback, and accompanied him — how far it is not said. This was often repeated until the spirit, becoming angry, refused any more to quit his disturber and continued to trouble him until 'Parson Jago' was called in to use his skill in laying Tucker's spirit to rest.

Three Jagos were at various times vicar of Wendron. This particular Parson Jago was noted not just for exorcism but for necromancy. He got into the habit of taking people to Wendron Cross and asking them whether they had a mind to see Tucker the man; he would make Tucker rise from the dead as a mark of particular favour to his acquaintances. The poor man, hounded by who knows what horrors in his life, was hounded in death first by a drunken farmer, then by a minister of the cloth overly proud of his powers.

The Hound of St Austell

Samuel Drew (1765-1833) was a self taught man of letters; his special interest was metaphysics, which is perhaps why he is little known now. He was apprenticed to a shoemaker, and gave the following account of a childhood experience.

'There were several of us, boys and men, out about twelve o'clock on a bright moonlit night. I think we were poaching. The party were in a field adjoining the road leading from my master's to St Austell, and I was stationed outside the hedge to watch and give the alarm if any intruder should appear. While thus occupied I heard what appeared to be the sound of a horse approaching from the town, and I gave a signal. My companions paused and came to the hedge where I was, to see the passenger [passer-by]. They looked through the bushes, and I drew myself close to the hedge, that I might not be observed. The sound increased and the supposed horseman seemed drawing near. The clatter of the hoofs became more and more distinct.

'We all looked to see who and what it was, and I was seized with a strange, indefinable feeling of dread; when, instead of a horse, there appeared, coming towards us, at an easy pace, but with the same sound that first caught my ear, a creature about the height of a large dog. It went close by me, and as it passed, it turned upon me and my companions huge fiery eyes that struck terror to all our hearts. The road where I stood branched off in two directions, in one of which there was a gate across. Towards the gate it moved, and, without any apparent obstruction, went on at its regular trot, which we heard several minutes after it had disappeared. Whatever it was, it put an end to our occupation, and we made the best of our way home.

'I have often endeavoured in later years, but without success, to account on natural principles for what I then heard and saw. As to the facts, I am sure there was no deception. It was a night of unusual brightness, occasioned by a cloudless full moon. The creature was unlike any animal I had then seen, but from my present recollections it had much the appearance of a bear, with a dark shaggy coat. Had it not been for the unearthly lustre of its eyes, and its passing through the gate as it did, there would be no reason to suppose it anything more than an animal escaped perhaps from some menagerie. That it did pass through the gate without pause or hesitation I am perfectly clear. Indeed, we all saw it, and saw that the gate was shut, from which we were not distant more than twenty or thirty yards. The bars were too close to admit the passage of an animal of half its apparent bulk; yet this creature went through without effort or variation of its pace.'

A ghost layer at work

A preacher living between Camborne and Helston in the mid-nineteenth century claimed to have put many troublesome spirits to rest, generally by settling for them their mundane affairs (such as small debts they died owing) or by reasoning with them that they should bear their punishment with a good heart, make the best of a bad job, and hope for better times. He admitted that sometimes he was merely deluding the ghosts; yet no matter, since the end sought was attained. Anything to get rid of them!

He told the sceptical William Bottrell, clearly in good faith, of one particular adventure. For some trifling reason the spirit got back to its late abode before the mourners had even left the pub in the church-town where, as is customary, they had stopped a while to take leave of their friends who had come from a distance.

The ghost became at once so annoying that none could rest in the house with it. A few nights after the burial, the family, not knowing what else to do to obtain any quiet, fetched the preacher, who was believed to possess extraordinary knowledge of spiritual matters and power over the ghostly world and its inhabitants. He entered the haunted house alone. After many hours passed in prayer and expostulation with the obstinate spirit, it at last consented to return to its grave and stay there, if the exorcist would accompany it to the churchyard to see it safely landed there.

And now happened the remarkable part of the affair. About midnight the ghost-layer bound the spirit with a piece of new rope, and fastened the other end of it round his own waist, that the spirit mightn't give him the slip. The spirit, gentle as a lamb, was then led out of the house; but it had no sooner crossed the doorsill than the dwelling was surrounded by a pack of yelping hounds, of which the town-place [farmyard] was full, and the Old One riding up the lane in a blaze of fire.

The spirit, to save itself from being caught by the diabolical hounds and huntsman, mounted high up in the air taking the man, hanging by his middle from the rope, with it. Away they went, over trees, hills and water. In less than a minute they passed over some three miles, and alighted in the churchyard, close by the spirit's grave, which the preacher saw open, and blue sulphurous flames issuing therefrom, and he heard, coming from below, most horrid shrieks and moans.

The ghost, knowing it was of no use contending with the man of faith, only stopped to say farewell and then descended into its grave, which immediately closed. The man — overcome by being borne with lightning speed through the air, or by the infernal fumes rising from the open grave — fell down in a fit from which he did not recover till daybreak, and then he was scarcely able to stagger from the churchyard. When near the town-place, which he had left with the spirit, he found in the branch of a tree his hat, which must have fallen from his head as they first mounted into the air.

The Admiral's wife

When Admiral Cotes was commanding a squadron in the East Indies he met with the following extraordinary incident. Retiring one night to his lodging room, he saw the form of his wife standing at his bedside, as plainly, he used to say, as he had ever seen her in England.

Greatly agitated, he hurried from the room and joined his brother officers, who had not yet retired to rest. But willing to persuade himself that this appearance was a mere illusion, he went again into his bedroom where he again saw his wife in the same attitude as before. She did not attempt to speak to him; but then slowly waved her hand and disappeared.

In the last letters he had received from England he was informed that his wife was perfectly well: his mind, in short, had been quite composed. Of this very singular occurrence, however, he immediately set down the particulars in his memorandum book, noting the exact time in which it happened. He saw also a minute made to the same purpose by several of his friends on board. The ship had begun her voyage homeward; so that before he could receive any intelligence from England, he arrived there; and on enquiry for his wife, he not only found that she was dead, but that she died at the very same hour of the night when her spirit appeared to him in the East Indies. This account the Admiral himself gave to the Rev. James Walker, vicar of Lanlivery; who had indeed seen the memorandum in the Admiral's pocket book, and who more than once related the above particulars.

Mary, wife of Admiral Thomas Cotes, died 22 March 1754, aged 35, and is buried at Lanlivery.

The ghostly duel

In the First World War there was a Royal Navy aerodrome constructed at Bonython on the Lizard, near Cury Cross Lanes, known as the Mullion Air Station. It was the base for airships used for anti-submarine warfare, convoy duties and observation, and of course the personnel were on virtually continuous duty except in weather which made flying impossible.

On one such day, 15 October 1917, Sub-Lieutenant A Jelf was given a short leave and walked towards Mullion to visit friends. He stopped on his way to look over a gate. In the field he saw, to his terror, a duel taking place, with the contestants apparently dressed in Stuart costumes, and armed with rapiers. One of the duellists was run through, and the seconds brought up a coffin, at which point the victor pointed his sword towards the flying officer who promptly fainted. When he came to he was on the ground by the gate: the field was empty, and he ran in a great panic, covered in mud, to his friends' house in Mullion.

It was assumed by them that he had suffered a hallucination as a result of excessive flying hours, but he remained convinced that the apparitions were supernatural. He wrote an account of his experience, which is in the Royal Institution library at Truro. Some years later, the local historian A S Oates met on a train a local vicar whom he knew, who tantalisingly said, 'By the way, was it you who told our mutual acquaintance Mr W. the story of the ghostly duel? You will be interested to know that the duel was again witnessed not long ago!' But at that point they arrived at Helston Station, where Mr Oates had to get off, and as the vicar immediately afterwards left Cornwall, he never found out the details of the second appearance of the duellists.

The spectre ship of Porthcurnow

A general belief once prevailed in the western parishes that in ancient times Parcurno (as it was known) was the principal port of Cornwall, and that until the cove became sanded up there was sufficient depth of water to float the largest ships then made in to the foot of an old caunce [paved road] which may still be seen. Spectre ships frequently visited Parcurno, both before and since its navigable channel filled with sand, and were often seen sailing up and down the valley, over dry land as well as over the sea. In olden times these naval apparitions were held to be 'tokens' that enemies were about to attack, the number of the vessels suggesting the scale of the marauding force.

In the early nineteenth century, the significance of the spectre ship, which by then was seen singly and never in convoy, had changed and become attached to the history of a family who lived at Chygwidden, a house a mile or so inland. Chygwidden had been the chief house of a family which flourished in St Levan for a few generations until all its branches became so reduced in circumstances, through riotous living, as to be obliged to sell or mortgage most of their lands.

The eldest and only son, by a former wife, of 'Old Martin' took to a sea-faring life, on account of cruel treatment received from his drunken father and a step-mother several years younger than himself. On leaving, he vowed that he would never return while she lived. Many years passed, and as no tidings had been received of Young Martin, as he was still called, most people believed him dead. In the meantime, his father, his step-mother and her children having all died within a few years of each other, a distant relative had taken possession of what little property remained, and lived at Chygwidden.

Some ten years after this, a large ship hove to within a mile of

Parcurno on a fine afternoon in harvest time. People working in fields near the cliff observed a boat leave the ship with two men, who landed in Parcurno with several chests and other goods; the ship proceeded on her course.

It was evident that one of those who came on shore was well acquainted with the place, as he struck at once into a pathway over the cliff which led by a short cut to Rospeltha, where he made himself known as Young Martin and procured horses and other help to take several heavy chests and bales to Chygwidden.

There was great rejoicing when it was known that the wanderer had at length returned to claim his own. His kinsfolk — a young man and his sister Eleanor, a damsel in her teens — were ready to resign possession, but Martin then cared little for house or land, and told them to keep the place and welcome, for all he desired was to have a home there for himself and his comrade whilst they remained, which he thought would only be for a short spell. His tastes had changed with change of scene. The place he had once deemed the fairest on earth — but then he had seen no more of it than was visible from the nearest high hill — now appeared dreary; and the people whom — those of his own family excepted — he once thought the best in the world now seemed a forlorn set of self-important grimly religious nobodies to him, and above all to his mate.

Martin found the people much altered from what they were in his youthful days, for about the time of his return a new sect had sprung up whose members, professing uncommon godliness, decried our ancient games and merry-makings, which were wont on holidays to unite all ages and classes. Their condemnation caused the old customs to fall into disuse; and, on account of the intolerant and censorious spirit which then prevailed, there was much less heartiness and cordial intercourse amongst neighbours than formerly.

In a short time however, Martin, now generally known as 'The Captain', became reconciled — one can't say attached — to his native place and the 'humdrum West Country folks' as he styled them, who marvelled at his riches and the change which had taken place in his outward manner. Yet the homely people's surprise at the alteration in Martin was nothing to their wonder, allied to fear, excited by his dark-skinned companion — or slave, for no one knew in what relation they stood to each other.

The stranger was seen to be robust, about thirty years of age apparently, with a complexion many shades darker than the Captain's mahogany tinted skin. Martin called this man José, or 'mate', and he rarely spoke a word of English (though he could when he pleased) or addressed anyone other than Martin, with whom he always conversed in some outlandish tongue which seemed more natural to the Captain than his mother tongue. A tantalising mystery shrouded the dark 'outlander'; for his master or friend would never answer any question respecting him. He was almost equally silent with regard to buccaneering or other adventures, and rarely spoke of anything that occurred either at home or abroad during his absence. The two strange beings often came to high words or even to blows, but they would never allow anyone to meddle in their quarrels. When Martin was drunk and off his guard, he would now and then ease his mind by swearing at his mate in plain English, or grumble at him that he had risked his life and spent a fortune to save him from being hanged at the yard-arm. 'Discontented devil,' he would say, 'why canst thou not be satisfied to live here? Thou art bound to me body and soul, and do I not indulge thee with everything gold can purchase?'

José would sometimes murmur, 'Avast there, all our gold and diamonds cannot procure us here the bright sunshine and joyous people, nor the rich fruits and wine, of my native clime.' He seldom, however, made any reply other than by gloomy looks or fiery glances which soon recalled Martin to his senses. It was remarked that after these outbursts of passion he was for a long while like the humble slave of his mate.

The boat in which they landed was kept at Parcurno, except for short spells during stormy times of the year when she was put into Penberth or Pargwartha for greater safety; and weeks together they would remain out at sea night and day till their provisions were used; then they would come in, their craft laden with fish, and this cargo was free to all comers. Stormy weather seldom drove them to land; they seemed to delight in a tempest.

Before winter came they procured a great number of hounds, and much of the hunting season was passed by them in coursing over all parts of the west. Often of winter's nights, people far away would be frightened by hearing or seeing these two wild-looking hunters and their dogs chasing over some lone moor, and they gave rise to many a story of Old Nick and his headless hounds.

When they tired of the chase, weeks were often passed at a public-house in Buryan Church-town. Martin treated one and all and scattered gold around him like chaff. The mate, however, at times restrained Martin's lavish expenditure, took charge of his money chests and refused him the keys.

José would occasionally condescend to express his wishes to Eleanor, who was the mistress of the rare establishment. She understood and humoured the pair, who took pleasure in decking her in the richest stuffs and jewels that their chests contained or that money could procure, and she frequently stayed up the best part of the night alone to await their return.

After being at home a year or so, the Captain had a large half-decked boat built, and several rocks removed in Parcurno to make a safer place in which to moor her. They then took longer trips and were not seen in Chygwidden for many months running. The two eccentric beings passed many years in this way, and held but little intercourse with their neighbours.

At length Martin perceived tokens of approaching death, or what he took for such, and made his man swear that when he appeared near to death he would take him off to sea, let him die there, and send him to his rest on the ocean's bottom. He also bound his kinsman by oath not to oppose his wishes and invoked a curse on anyone who would lay his dust beside the remains of those who had driven him to range the wide world like a vagabond.

They might have complied with his strange desires, but before they could be carried out he died, in a hammock suspended in his bedroom.

Now comes the mystery. It is certain that a coffin, followed by the cousins, José and the dogs, was taken to St Levan churchyard and buried near the ground in which Martin's family lie. But it was rumoured that the coffin merely contained earth to make weight. The following night the outlander had two chests conveyed to Parcurno, the larger of which was said to contain the remains of his friend, and the other money and valuables which belonged to himself. The chests were placed on board the half-decked vessel, José and his favourite dog embarked, waited for the tide to rise and put to sea; but no one remained at the cove to witness their departure and no more was seen in the West of man, dog or boat.

Eleanor disappeared on the funeral night and it was surmised that she left with the stranger, who was scarcely a league to sea when a tempest arose and continued with great fury for nearly a week; and although it was winter, the sky of nights was all ablaze with lightning and the days as dark as nights. During this storm, Parcurno was choked with sand and no boat could be kept there since.

The tempest had scarcely lulled when an apparition of Martin's craft would drive into Parcurno against wind and tide; oft-times she came in the dusk of evening and without stopping at the cove took her course up over the old caunce to Chapel Curnow; thence she sailed away, her keel just skimming the ground or many yards above it, as she passed over hill and dale till she arrived at Chygwidden. The barque was generally shrouded in mist and one could rarely get a glimpse of her deck on which the shadowy figures of two men, a woman and a dog were now and then beheld. This ship of the dead, with her ghostly crew, hovered over Chygwidden town-place a moment, then bore away to a croft on the farm and vanished near a rock where a large sum of foreign coins was disinterred many years ago, so it is said. Since the laying of the Atlantic telegraph cable from Parcurno, the ship has not been seen, and may never more be so in that ancient port.

The Keigwin Arms, Mousehole

The picturesque old mansion of the Keigwins is now [1870] transformed into a public house. No wonder for these old gentry to be uneasy in their graves (as Mousehole people all know they are) to find their grand old mansion so degraded. Any person in the town will tell you that there is scarcely a night but, at the usual hour for ghosts to leave their graves, these unresting old gentry revisit their family home and there hold a revel-rout best part of the night. There is such a noisy getting up and down stairs with the ghostly gentlemen's boots creaking and stamping, spurs and swords jingling, ladies' silks rustling and their hoops striking the banisters, that the living inmates get but little rest before cock-crow, when they betake themselves off. Sometimes these unwelcome visitors vary their fun by knocking about the furniture, smashing the glasses, having a dance, etc; altogether they seem to be a right merry set of ghosts, yet they often succeed in making the tenants quit the house, as few persons like to have their sleep disturbed by such troublesome visitors.

The demeanour of the spirits of these old Keigwins is altogether different from that of well-behaved, serious, Christian ghosts; indeed they have at particular times made so much disturbance that no person in the house could get a wink of sleep, and, that they might be sent off if only for a time, the living inmates have had recourse to preachers and other pious folks; and they say that by their singing, praying and other religious exercises, they have sometimes succeeded in driving these uneasy spirits from the house for the time. Not many years ago — within the memory of scores now at Mousehole, the public house being then kept by J.R. — these nocturnal disturbances were renewed; the leaders and deacons of the society, and good men of the town, were called in and, whilst T.R.

and J.W. were praying, those untoward spirits kept on at their ghostly work of knocking and throwing about the chairs and other furniture, regardless of praying men. They were, however, shamed and silenced for a while; but all the parson-power in the country, it is believed, would not be sufficient to put them to rest effectually.

One night not long ago, the mistress of the house heard a noise in the large parlour, as if the chairs and tables were having a dance as well as the ghosts. This was followed by such a crash of breaking glass as if all the contents of the corner-buffet were dashed on the floor. The fear that all her beautiful old china and glass were gone to smash drove away all other dread, and the mistress ventured down, candle in hand, to see what was going on; but when she ventured into the room, she saw that the furniture was exactly as left when she went to bed. The curious glasses, with twisted stems, and china punch-bowls were all safe and sound in the buffet. Believing then that there was no one but herself in the lower part of the house, she was proceeding to go upstairs when, happening to cast a glance towards the broad landing, she saw a number of gentlemen and ladies ascending the stairs in great state — the ladies decked out in all the pride of hoops and fardingales, the gentlemen in laced coats, swords and funnel top boots, with their rattling spurs; in fact they were all equipped as they appeared in their old pictures which were to be seen in some rooms of the ancient mansion a few years ago.

Dorothy Dingley - the Botathan ghost

The following story, described by more than one writer as the best ghost story in English, has a surprising publishing history. It first appeared in June 1720 in *Mr Campbell's Pacquet for the Entertainment of Gentlemen and Ladies*, a pamphlet which was soon afterwards bound into the second edition of *History of the Life and Adventures of Mr Duncan Campbell*. Duncan Campbell was a Scot, deaf and dumb, but apparently gifted with the second sight, who was at that time making a fashionable success in London. The instant biography was 'by the author of Robinson Crusoe', namely Daniel Defoe, taking advantage of his new-found fame and that of Mr Campbell.

Defoe frequently wrote fiction as first person narratives (Robinson Crusoe himself and Moll Flanders being the most famous examples) and it was for long assumed that he had written this narrative. Hawker of Morwenstow then re-used the tale for his own purposes, muddled the facts and introduced a great deal of mumbo-jumbo. But in the 1890s, Alfred Robbins proved conclusively that the story was what it claimed to be — a genuine narrative, by Rev. Dr John Ruddle, who had been vicar of Launceston from 1663 to 1699, and that the events occurred in the parish of South Petherwin, two miles south-west of Launceston.

Since the narrative is genuine, we have reproduced it virtually unedited and hope readers will not find the style of a seventeenth century parson too difficult to read. Further historical details will be found at the end of the story.

A remarkable passage of an apparition,
Related by the Rev. Dr Ruddle
of Launceston in Cornwall, in the year 1665

In the beginning of this year a disease happened in this town of Launceston, and some of my scholars died of it. Among others who fell under the malignity then triumphing, was John Eliot, the eldest son of Edward Eliot of Treherse, Esq., a stripling of about sixteen years of age, but of more than common parts and ingenuity. At his own particular request I preached at the funeral, which happened on the 20th day of June 1665. In my discourse I spoke some words in commendation of the young gentleman; such as might endear his memory to those who knew him and, withal, tended to preserve his example to the fry which went to school with him, and were to continue there after him.

An ancient gentleman who was then in the church was much affected with this discourse and was often heard to repeat, the same evening, an expression I then used out of Vergil:

et puer ipse fuit cantari dignus
[Now, *there* was a boy worth a eulogy.]

The reason why this grave gentleman was so concerned at the character was a reflection he made upon a son of his own who, being about the same age and a few months before not unworthy of the like character I gave the young Mr Eliot, was now by a strange accident quite lost as to his parent's hopes and all expectation of further comfort by him.

The funeral rites being over, I was no sooner come out of the church but I found myself most courteously accosted by this old gentleman; and with an unusual importunity, almost forced against my humour to see his house that night; nor could I have rescued myself from his kindness, had not Mr Eliot interposed and pleaded title to me for the whole of the day, which, as he said, he would resign to no man. Here upon I got loose for that time, but was constrained to leave a promise behind me to wait upon him at his own house the Monday following. This then seemed to satisfy, but before Monday came I had a new message to request me that, if it were possible, I would be there on the Sunday. The second attempt I resisted, by answering that it was against my convenience, and the duty which mine own people expected from me. Yet the gentleman was not at rest, for he sent me another letter on the Sunday, by no means to fail on the Monday, and so to order my business as to spend two or three days with him at least. I was indeed startled at so much eagerness, and so many dunnings for a visit, without any business; and began to suspect that there must needs be some design in the bottom of all this excess of courtesy. For I had no familiarity, scarce common acquaintance with the gentleman or his family; nor could I imagine whence should arise such a flush of friendship on the sudden.

On the Monday I went and paid my promised devoir, and met with entertainment as free and plentiful as the invitation was importunate. There also I found a neighbouring minister who pretended to call in accidentally, but by the sequel I suppose it otherwise. After dinner this brother of the coat undertook to show me the gardens, where, as we were walking, he gave me the first discovery of what was mainly intended in all this treat and compliment.

First he began to tell the infortunity of the family in general, and then gave an instance in the youngest son. He related what a hopeful, sprightly lad he lately was, and how melancholic and sottish he was now grown. Then did he with much passion lament, that his ill-humour should so incredibly subdue his reason; for, says he, the poor boy believes himself to be haunted with ghosts, and is confident that he meets with an evil spirit in a certain field about half a mile from this place, as often as he goes that way to school.

In the midst of our twaddle, the old gentleman and his lady (as observing their cue exactly) came up to us. Upon their approach, and pointing me to the arbour, the parson renews the relation to me; and they (the parents of the youth) confirmed what he said and added many minute circumstances in a long narrative of the whole. They all three desired my thoughts and advice in the affair.

I was not able to collect thoughts enough on the sudden to frame a judgement of what they had said, only I answered, that the thing which the youth reported to them was strange, yet not incredible, and that I knew not then what to think or say of it; but if the lad would be free to me in talk, and trust me with his counsels, I had hopes to give them a better account of my opinion the next day.

I had no sooner spoken so much, but I perceived myself in the springe [trap] their courtship had laid for me; for the old lady was not able to hide her impatience, but her son must be called immediately. This I was forced to comply with and consent to, so that drawing off from the company to an orchard near by, she went herself and brought him to me, and left him with me.

It was the main drift of all these three to persuade me that either the boy was lazy, and glad of any excuse to keep from the school, or that he was in love with some wench and ashamed to confess it; or that he had a fetch [stratagem] upon his father to get money and new clothes, that he might range to London after a brother he had there; and thereupon they begged me to discover the root of the matter, and accordingly to dissuade, advise or reprove him, but chiefly, by all means, to undeceive him as to the fancy of ghosts and spirits.

I soon entered into a close conference with the youth, and at first was very cautious not to displease him, but by smooth words to ingratiate myself and get within him, for I doubted he would be too distrustful or reserved. But we had scarcely passed the first situation, and begun to speak to the business, before I found that there needed no policy to screw myself into his breast; for he most openly, and with all-obliging candour did aver, that he loved his book and desired nothing more than to be bred a scholar; that he had not the least respect for [attachment to] any of womankind, as his mother gave out; and that the only request he would make to his parents was, that they would but believe his constant assertions concerning the woman he was disturbed with, in the field called the Higher-Broom Quartils. He told me with all naked freedom and a flood of tears that his friends [close relatives] were unkind and unjust to him, neither to believe nor pity him; and that if any man (making a bow to me) would but go with him to the place, he might be convinced that the thing was real.

By this time he found me apt to compassionate his condition, and to be attentive of his relation of it, and therefore he went on in this way:

'This woman which appears to me,' saith he, 'lived a neighbour here to my father, and died about eight years since; her name Dorothy Dingley, of such a stature, such age, and such complexion. She never speaks to me but passeth by hastily, and always leaves the footpath to me, and she commonly meets me twice or three times in the breadth of the field.

'It was about two months before I took any notice of it, and though the shape of the face was in my memory, yet I did not recall the name of the person, but without more thoughtfulness I did suppose it was some woman who lived thereabout, and had frequent occasion that way. Nor did I imagine anything to the contrary before she began to meet me constantly, morning and evening, and always in the same field, and sometimes twice or thrice in the breadth of it.

'The first time I took notice of her was about a year since, and when I first began to suspect and believe it to be a ghost, I had courage enough not to be afraid, but kept it to myself a good while, and only wondered very much about it. I did often speak to it but never had a word in answer. Then I changed my way and went to school the Under Horse Road, and then she always met me in the narrow lane, between the Quarry Park and the Nursery, which was worse.

'At length I began to be terrified at it, and prayed continually that God would either free me or let me know the meaning of it. Night and day, sleeping and waking, the shape was ever running in my mind, and I did often repeat that place of Scripture (with that he takes a small bible out of his pocket), Job vii, 14: "Thou scarest me with dreams and terrifiest me through visions".'

I was very much pleased with the lad's ingenuity in the application of this scripture pertinent to his condition, and desired him to proceed.

'When,' says he, 'by degrees I grew very pensive, inasmuch that it was taken notice of by all our family; whereupon, being urged to it, I told my brother William of it, and he privately acquainted my father and mother, and they kept it to themselves for some time.

'The success of this discovery was only this; they did sometimes laugh at me, sometimes chide me but still commanded me to keep to my school and put such fopperies out of my head. I did accordingly go to school often, but always met the woman in the way.'

This and much more to the same purpose, yea, as much as held a dialogue of nearly two hours, was our conference in the orchard, which ended in my proffer to him, that, without making any privy to our intents, I would next morning walk with him to the place, about six o'clock. He was even transported with joy at the mention of it, and replied, 'But will you, sure, sir? Thank God! Now I hope I shall be relieved.' From this conclusion we retired into the house.

The gentleman, his wife and my brother minister were impatient to know the event, insomuch that they came out of the parlour into the hall to meet us; and seeing the lad look cheerfully, the first compliment from the old man was, 'Come, Mr Ruddle, you have talked with him; I hope he will now have more wit. An idle boy! an idle boy!' At these words the lad ran upstairs to his own chamber without replying, and I soon stopped the curiosity of the three expectants by telling them that I had promised silence, and was resolved to be as good as my word; but when things were riper they might know all. At present, I desired them to rest in my faithful promise, that I would do my utmost in their service, and for the good of their son. With this they were silenced; I cannot say satisfied.

The next morning before five o'clock, the lad was in my chamber and very brisk. I arose and went with him. The field he led me to I guessed to be twenty acres, in an open country and about three furlongs from any house. We went into the field and had not gone above a third part, before the spectrum, in the shape of a woman, with all the circumstances he had described her to me in the orchard the day before (as much as the suddenness of its appearance and evanition [vanishing] would permit me to discover) met us and passed by. I was a little surprised at it, and though I had taken up a firm resolution to speak to it, yet I had not the power, nor indeed durst I look back; yet I took care not to show any fear to my pupil and guide, and therefore only telling him that I was satisfied in the truth of his complaint, we walked to the end of the field and returned, nor did the ghost meet us that time above once. I perceived in the young man a kind of boldness, mixed with astonishment; the first caused by my presence and the proof he had given of his own relation, and the other by the sight of his persecutor.

In short we went home: I somewhat puzzled, he much animated. At our return, the gentlewoman, whose inquisitiveness had missed us, watched to speak with me. I told her that my opinion was that her son's complaint was not to be slighted, nor altogether discredited; yet that my judgement in his case was not settled. I gave her caution, moreover, that the thing might not take wind, lest the whole country should ring with something we had as yet no assurance of.

In this juncture of time I had business which would admit no delay; wherefore I went for Launceston that evening, but promised to see them again next week. Yet I was prevented by an occasion which pleaded a sufficient excuse, for my wife was that week brought home from a neighbour's house very ill. However, my mind was upon the adventure. I studied the case, and about three weeks later went again, resolving, by the help of God, to see the utmost.

The next morning, being the 27th day of July 1665, I went to the haunted field by myself, and walked the breadth of the field without any encounter. I returned and took the other walk, and then the spectrum appeared to me, much about the same place where I saw it before, when the young gentleman was with me. In my thoughts, it moved swifter than the time before, and about ten feet distance from me upon my right hand, insomuch that I had not time to speak, as I had determined with myself beforehand.

The evening of this day, the parents, the son and myself being in the chamber where I lay, I propounded to them our going all to the place next morning, and after some asseveration [assurances] that there was no danger in it, we all resolved upon it. The morning being come, lest we should alarm the family of servants, they went under the pretence of seeing a field of wheat, and I took my horse and fetched my compass another way, and so we met at the stile we had appointed.

Thence we all four walked leisurely into the Quartils, and had passed above half the field before the ghost made appearance. It then came over the stile just before us, and moved with that swiftness that by the time we had gone six or seven steps, it had passed by. I immediately turned head and ran after it, with the young man by my side; we saw it pass over the stile by which we entered, but no farther. I stepped upon the hedge at one place, he at another, but could discern nothing; whereas I dare aver, that the swiftest horse in England could not have conveyed himself out of sight in that short space of time. Two things I observed in this day's appearance. 1. That a spaniel dog, who followed the company unregarded, did bark and run away, as the spectrum passed by; whence it is easy to conclude that it was not our fear or fancy that made the apparition. 2. That the motion of the spectrum was not by gradation, or by steps, and moving of the feet, but a kind of gliding, as children upon the ice, or a boat down a swift river, which punctually answers the description the ancients gave of their *lemures* [Latin for ghosts].

But to proceed. This ocular evidence clearly convinced but, withal, strangely frightened the old gentleman and his wife, who knew this Dorothy Dingley in her lifetime, were at her burial, and now plainly saw her features in this present apparition. I encouraged them as well as I could, but after this they went no more. However, I was resolved to proceed, and use such lawful means as God hath discovered, and learned men have successfully practised in these irregular cases.

The next morning being Thursday, I went out very early by myself, and walked for about an hour's space in meditation and prayer in the field next adjoining to the Quartils. Soon after five I stepped over the stile into the disturbed field, and had not gone above thirty or forty paces before the ghost appeared at the further stile. I spoke to it with a loud voice, in some such sentences as the way of these dealings directed me; whereupon it approached, but slowly, and when I came near, it moved not. I spake again, and it answered, in a voice neither very audible nor intelligible. I was not in the least terrified, and therefore persisted until it spake again, and gave me satisfaction. But the work could not be finished at this time; wherefore, the same evening, an hour before sunset, it met me again near the same place, and after a few words on each side, it quietly vanished, and neither doth appear since, nor ever will more to any man's disturbance. The discourse in the morning lasted about a quarter of an hour.

These things are true, and I know them to be so, with as much certainty as eyes and ears can give me; and until I can be persuaded that my senses do deceive me about their proper object, and by that persuasion deprive myself of the strongest inducement to believe the Christian religion, I must and will assert that these things in this paper are true.

Some facts in the story can be cross-checked: John Eliot, son of Edward and Anne Eliot of Trebursye, was indeed buried at South Petherwin church on the day stated, according to the Parish Register. Ruddle's wife was indeed ill, and died two years later. The boy's route to the school in Launceston would indeed have taken him through a lane past 'Quarry Park'.

Other facts were concealed by the author, as is often the case in 'genuine' ghost stories, to protect families from scandal or ridicule, or avoid libel action — making it hard to tell 'genuine' stories from purely fictional. These facts were discovered by research in the 1890s. The haunted family were the Blighs of Botathan in South Petherwin, where there was then still a Higher Broom Field, though it is no longer so called. Thomas Bligh, the father, was a neighbour and friend of Edward Eliot. Local tradition says Dorothy was a maid-servant at Botathan, who had been the mistress either of Thomas Bligh or his elder son, and that she died in childbirth.

A copy of the manuscript still existed at Launceston a hundred years ago, perhaps still does. So how did Defoe get hold of a copy? Defoe visited Launceston in 1705, touring Devon and Cornwall as a spy for the MI5 of his day, looking for signs of revolt and possibly acting as an *agent provocateur.* Since he found that the Cornish boroughs in which he stayed were entirely under the thumb of local gentry who were government supporters, with no budding revolutionaries, he had ample time to follow his other interests, including the paranormal; presumably he retained a copy of Ruddle's narrative for fifteen years, before it suited him to publish.

One fact in Parson Ruddle's manuscript is false; his contention that Dorothy would never again disturb the inhabitants of Botathan — for she does so to this day.

The Stockadon spider

More than a hundred years ago [written in 1929] Stockadon Farm on the banks of the Lynher, in the parish of Southill, was the scene of a midnight supper given to four parsons.

An unfortunate occurrence had made this necessary. A girl apprentice, running to escape a beating at the farmer's hands, had attempted to cross the Lynher which ran near the farm and was drowned, whereupon she at once became troublesome as a spirit. For example, when her master returned from seeing her 'drowned dead', so to speak, behold she was back at the farm driving the geese! Which was not very pleasant for the farmer.

And that was not all. Things finally got to such a pitch that four parsons — perhaps more, but certainly no fewer — were summoned to lay the ghost. They sat down to a specially prepared supper and between midnight and one o'clock in the morning the spirit appeared.

The upshot of it was that the spirit was 'bound' as a spider in a cupboard by the fireplace, and the shut cupboard was papered over and left strictly alone — until about 47 years ago [1882]. A woman who was in service at Stockadon under the grandson of the farmer in question remembers the cupboard well. It was not papered over in her time, though always shut; it looked much as it does now, a full-sized door by the fireplace in the room to the left of the front entrance to the house. Behind the door are four or five narrow shelves. But the girl and her fellow servants never dared open it: they were afraid. Did they imagine the spider still there, listening?

Of course the cupboard did not remain unopened, and nothing at all was found in it, except spiders.

A Providential Ghost

The following letter, dated Redruth, 22 January 1784, appeared in the Arminian Magazine, then the leading journal of the Methodists, in the issue of December 1785. The spelling of place names has been left unchanged.

A few days ago I visited John Thomas, of St Just in Cornwall. He is about sixty-two years of age and has been a notorious drunkard, the greatest part of his life.

He told me that on Sunday December 21, 1783, about seven o'clock in the evening, he left St Crete in order to go to St Just's. That, as it was dark, he missed his way, and about midnight fell into a pit about five fathoms deep.

On his being missed, his friends made diligent search for him, but to no purpose. The next Sabbath-day, as one of his neighbours was going to seek his sheep, he saw at some distance the appearance of a man sitting on a bank which had been thrown up in digging the pit. On drawing near, he saw the apparition going round to the other side of the bank. When he came to the place, he could see no one; but heard a human voice in the bottom of the pit. Thinking that some smugglers had got down the pit to hide their liquors, he went on; but coming back the same way, he again heard the voice. He now listened more attentively; and as he could hear but one voice, he concluded it was John Thomas, who was missing; and on calling him he found he was not mistaken. On this he went to get help, and soon got him out of the pit. As he had been there near eight days, he was very low when he was got out; but is now in a fair way to do well.

In the bottom of the pit he found a small current of water, which he drank very freely of; this, in all likelihood, was the means of keeping him alive. It is said that several other persons saw the apparition but took no notice of it.

As I am not fond of crediting stories of this kind on common report, I resolved to get the account from his own mouth.

William Moore

The Black Bull of Mylor

In compiling this little book, I have had occasion to read many old collections of ghost stories: among the conventions of the genre, one is to include as the last story a tale of an animal ghost. Perhaps theological doubts about whether animals have souls make the ghost of an animal even more questionable than the ghost of a person and condemns them to the final chapter? Anyway, here is a Cornish animal ghost story, told by an old lady in the 1890s.

When I was a little girl in Mylor, I used to live down in one of the cottages beside the beach, just below Portloe, with my mother and my step-father, who was one of the coastguards. In them days there used to be a ship come over to France every so often for oysters, and the ship used to lay up in Mylor Creek. There were two coastguards kept, because there used to be a brave bit of smuggling carried on, on the quiet. Mother and me, and my step-father, lived in one of these two cottages, and the other coastguard and his wife lived in the other.

One night the two men were out on their rounds, and were intending to make their way towards Trefusis Point, so as to pass by the Big Zoon, when after they had passed the church stile, they were suddenly brought to a stop. Away in the distance, coming towards them, they could hear a fearful roaring noise; then they could hear the gravel flying, and as the sound came nearer they could make out the form of a big black bull, tearing towards them with fire coming from his nostrils, and roaring something terrible!

They took and runned back towards the churchyard and got in behind the wall, and when the bull passed by they both fired their pistols right at him; but they might just so well have spit at him for all the use it was! — anyhow, they took on after the bull, and it kept on running over the beach below Lawithick. At last we indoors could hear the noise. We two and the neighbour came out to see what was on, but we went back pretty quick! The houses were shaking as the bull passed by and he went away up the road with the men after him till after passing Well Ackett, and there they lost all sight of him and at last came back again.

The next day they sent round to the different parishes but nobody had lost a black bull, nor heard of one being lost.